Mama,
Enjoy the book ... the first
of many, I hope. 😊 ♡ Johanna
2009

# CABO & CORAL'S SECRET SURF SPOT!

By Dr. Udo Wahn

Illustrated by Hanna Daly

Copyright 2009 by Dr. Udo Wahn
Library of Congress Control Number:  2009903940
ISBN: 978-0-692-00269-8
1st Edition

This book was printed in Singapore by Craft Print International Ltd.
Art production: Hang 5 Art & Graphics
www.hang5art.com

To order additional copies of this book or Cabo and Coral Go Surfing! contact:
Dr. Udo Wahn

Author and publisher of books with aloha for the ocean–minded child

udo@caboandcoral.com
www.caboandcoral.com

# Dedication

I dedicate this book to my parents and in-laws, Frieda and Erich Wahn, and Anne and Ernie Kreitz, who have since passed on. My wife Aleida, and son, Paolo "Cabo" and I, along with other family members, will carry the torch from here.

*"Individually, we are one drop. Together, we are an ocean."*

- Ryunosuke Satoro

# Acknowledgements

A huge **thank you** to the following:

My dear friend and mentor **Bill Spore** who has guided me on a number of Baja surf trip adventures and misadventures.

**Brian Galt**, Hang 5 Art & Graphics, for his amazing talent as a graphic artist creating the cover design and book layout.

**Jay Thomas** for coming up with the name Slim. **Terri Thomas**, for your encouragement and review of the manuscript.

**Viva Sterner** and **Deborah Pagliaccio**, are teachers and family members, who reviewed the manuscript and gave me sound advice. Kudos to you.

**Steve** and **Jill Winters**, **Lea**, **Gina** and **Andres Spagarino**, and **Kimera** and **Brigette Hobbs** for their stoke upon reading the manuscript after our New Year's Day Polar Bear Plunge event in Del Mar 2009 and for encouraging me to go on writing this book.

**"Miguel"** of the "Fish house" at the campground. You know who you are! I appreciate your brisk sales of the Cabo and Coral Go Surfing!

**Reef Check Foundation** for their support of this book. The foundation is an international non-profit organization dedicated to the conservation of two ecosystems: tropical coral reefs and California rocky reefs. www.reefcheck.org

**The Rob Machado Foundation** for supporting this project and for helping kids understand their contribution toward a healthy earth. www.robmachadofoundation.org

My wife, **Aleida**, for finding Hanna to do the illustrations, naming Coral and keeping things running smoothly at home.

School's out for summer! Cabo's parents, Slim and Layla, have invited Cabo's friend Coral to take an adventurous surf trip along the coast. They load the surfboards on top of the funky old van that has been converted from gas to run on electricity. This new type of power will help keep the air cleaner and our earth from getting too warm.

Along the way, Cabo and Coral are reading surf magazines when all of a sudden they come around the bend in the windy road and see something incredible.

5

Off in the distance they see perfect aqua-colored waves that are breaking into a secluded cove nestled by a forest of tall trees.

6

"Dad, let's stop and catch a few waves," says Cabo.
"Ok." says Slim.
"We can surf and then have a yummy picnic lunch on the beach," says Layla.

They all watch the crashing surf for a while, getting a sense of how big the lumbering set waves are before paddling out. They watch carefully to see where the local surfers enter the ocean.

Once they have made it out
beyond the breakers,
they smile and say " Aloha!"
to the surfers that are
already surfing. They wait
in the brilliant sunshine and
toasty warm water to take
their turn to surf.

Coral catches the first wave of a
four wave set.
She has a great ride and pulls off
some fun surf tricks.
Cabo goes next followed by Layla
hanging five, and finally Slim.
Their new friends in the lineup
cheer them on!

After their picnic among the fragrant grove of trees,
they start driving to Slim and Layla's favorite campground
on the beach.
Along the way they come to what looks like a
dry riverbed winding below lush green hills that are
splashed with the vibrant colors of wildflowers.

Slim decides to take a short cut across to the
road that has looped around the riverbed.

Maybe that's not the best idea.

Halfway across the riverbed, the van sinks into the chocolate-colored gooey mud, which is hidden beneath the dry crispy surface. "This was a bonehead idea!" exclaims Slim in dismay. Luckily, a farmer named Kailani, uses his tractor to pull them out of the mucky mess to the firm road on the other side.

14

Slim wants to give Kailani something to show his appreciation for his help but Kailani does not want to accept anything. Kailani simply says, "Aloha my friend!"

It is very clear to everyone that taking a short cut isn't always the best choice.

Just when Cabo and Coral are about to ask, "Are we there yet?" the alluring smell of the sea fills the van. From the hilltop they see the broad sandy beach on the wild isolated coastline. Everyone gasps when they see the raw beauty of the setting.

"Wow! A campground on the beach." shout Cabo and Coral together.

Miguel's Fish House

Early the next morning they grab their boards and
hike for quite a way down the seashell strewn beach
to a popular surf spot called Spider Reef.
Layla says, "There are a bunch of people out surfing.
Let's have a look around the bluff and see how the
surf looks further down the beach."

By this time they all were getting pretty tired of carrying their boards and walking in the soft sand, but they keep going. Just around the point and over some gnarly rocks they are surprised at what they find . . .

. . . a dream come true!

There are beautiful head high waves peeling
into the cove and nobody is out in the water.
The sight of playful dolphins, breaching whales
and hungry squawking seabirds bring huge
smiles to the adventurers' faces.

21

After surfing this magical spot, Coral enthusiastically says to Cabo,
"Those were the longest rides I've ever had! This place is sweet."
Later they ask a local surfer if this surf spot has a name.
The surfer says with a smile, "It doesn't have a name . . . yet."

Cabo quickly reacts and asks his dad, "Is it cool if we call this surf spot Bonehead Point?"
Everyone roars with laughter!

After a blazing sunset, night arrives. "Look at that sparkling sky! This is amazing! There's the Milky Way" says Coral.
They all look up and also see the Big and Little Dippers among the millions of other bright stars that appear like glittering diamonds.

24

They tell jokes and stories as they stare into the dancing flames of the campfire and roast marshmallows to end a great day.

The next morning, they wake up to see a boat anchored above a deep water reef. It turns out that there are divers from Reef Check planting kelp and monitoring the different types and numbers of fish on the reef. They compare their findings year after year to be sure the reef stays healthy.

The surf is pretty small today, so they decide to walk along the beach and over to the river mouth. They are saddened to see all the plastic bags and bottles that have been washed down the river and onto the beach. "Yuck!" says Coral.

Slim reminds everyone of the Surfrider Foundation motto, to "Rise above plastic."
He also reminds them of the three R's: reduce, reuse and recycle. As they clean up the beach other people come by to help.

29

They return to the campsite, where
they clean up and make sure to leave
only their footprints in the sand.
They gather together to take one
last photo before driving back
home. Everyone agrees to keep
Bonehead Point a secret.
It would be their secret surf spot!

Aloha!

31

# The Surfrider Foundation 'Rise Above Plastic' Pledge

I commit to do my part to rise above plastics and protect the world's oceans, waves and beaches from plastic pollution. I will do this by:
- Using reusable bottles for my water and other drinks. By using just one reusable bottle, I will keep 167 single-use plastic bottles from entering the environment.
- Using cloth bags for groceries and other purchases. For each reusable bag I use, I will save approximately 400 plastics from being used.
- Recycling the plastic bags and bottles I already have. For every thirteen plastic bags I don't use, I will save enough petroleum to drive a car one mile.

**Udo** in search of waves on the road to Nosara, Costa Rica. Udo is an active core volunteer for Surfrider Foundation, San Diego chapter. He enjoys travel with the family, surfing, mountain biking and running on the beach. He has still been known to "catch" a few babies from time to time!

**Hanna Daly** creating the illustrations that gave vibrant life to my story. Hanna is a muralist living in San Diego. As you can tell from her art, she loves the ocean, swimming and scuba diving. "Bringing Cabo and Coral's Secret Surf Spot! to life was a wonderful experience." She dedicates these paintings to her awesome kids, KC and Dexter. Her website is a great place to check out her vast portfolio of artwork. www.HannasMurals.com.

My son, **Paolo "Cabo"** at age 5 exploring the tide pools at the beach in Del Mar, California. One of the happiest kids on earth! Paolo you bring great joy to me and your mom. We love you!

My wife, **Aleida**, as a child at play in her birthplace, Bolivia. This photo inspired the creation of the character, "Coral".